Disney
Fancy NANCY

Coloring &
Activity Book

Meet Nancy. She's very fancy.

Written by Nancy Parent

Illustrated by the Disney Storybook Art Team

endon®

e BENDON name, logo and
r and Share are trademarks of
don, Inc., Ashland, OH 44805.

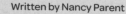

I love my family—even if they are kind of plain.

Voilà! My dog, Frenchy, looks better with a little sparkle.

Ooh la la, how fancy!
My best friend, Bree, and I love to dress up.

Nancy's Fancy

Nancy has some pretty fancy dreams.
Draw what she is dreaming about inside the frame.

Oh, no! The butterfly's wings got wet.

"I will call you *Papillon*," I say.
That's French for butterfly.

Bree and I can see that *Papillon's* wings are not working.

Let's Count!

Count each of the hats and boas on Nancy's coatrack.

Answer: 12

We don't want to scare *Papillon*.
So we dress up like butterflies.

"Let's make *Papillon* feel at home," says Bree.

Voilà! I think of the perfect house for *Papillon*.

Who Could It Be?

Connect the dots to meet Nancy's fancy new friend.

We make *Papillon's* house very fancy.

I imagine *Papillon* at a tea party.

"That tickles, *Papillon*!" I say.

Hidden Friends

Circle the eight hidden butterflies
in Nancy's garden.

I imagine that *Papillon* and I take flight.

Ooh la la! I have a new helper!

I see that *Papillon* needs to be
free to fly with the other butterflies.

Nancy Times Four

Circle the picture of Nancy that is different.

A

B

C

D

"*Au revoir, Papillon,*" I say. That's French for goodbye.

JoJo and Freddy have a secret pirate code. Use the number and letter key below to find out what they are saying!

___ ___ ___ ___ ___   ___ ___ ___ ___ ___ !
 1   3   5   7   4   1   6   2   7

A=1

E=2

H=3

M=4

O=5

T=6

Y=7

N

JoJo and her friend, Freddy, see Bree and I coming.

Arrrgggghhh! The pirates attack!

Find the line that leads to Rhonda and Wanda!

What's Different?

Circle six things that look different in the second scene.

Word Search Puzzle

```
F N E H K P S G Y C C I N D G
R D Q W F N Q A R L C Q O X T
E W K W N T M M L J T Z K H E
N M Q Q Q G K P O Y K E W J C
C X A Y D A D J O M L F H P P
H Y Y R Y W O W W O O B K M C
Y Y D O A N O F F I H C S U A
N A G D M B A B Z V F B M Y K
J M R X E Y E X T R N W U K P
J Q A Q H R D L Q Z A O Q X N
O G N D X A F D L X Y Z P G O
Z L D X K W Q E E E W A I E H
F R P N A N C Y O R J I P E G
Z L A X K W Q E E E W A I E H
P G A N W F R W H R F Y W R C
M A R A B E L L E I V T T B Y
```

Fancy Nancy's Friends and Family

NANCY   CHIFFON

BREE   FREDDY

JOJO

MOM

DAD

GRANDPA

FRENCHY

MARABELLE

Fancy Wordplay

How many words can you make from the word playhouse?
Write them below. Here are some examples: hop, pal, lap.

I want to have a dog show in my backyard.

Find the leash that leads to Jewel.

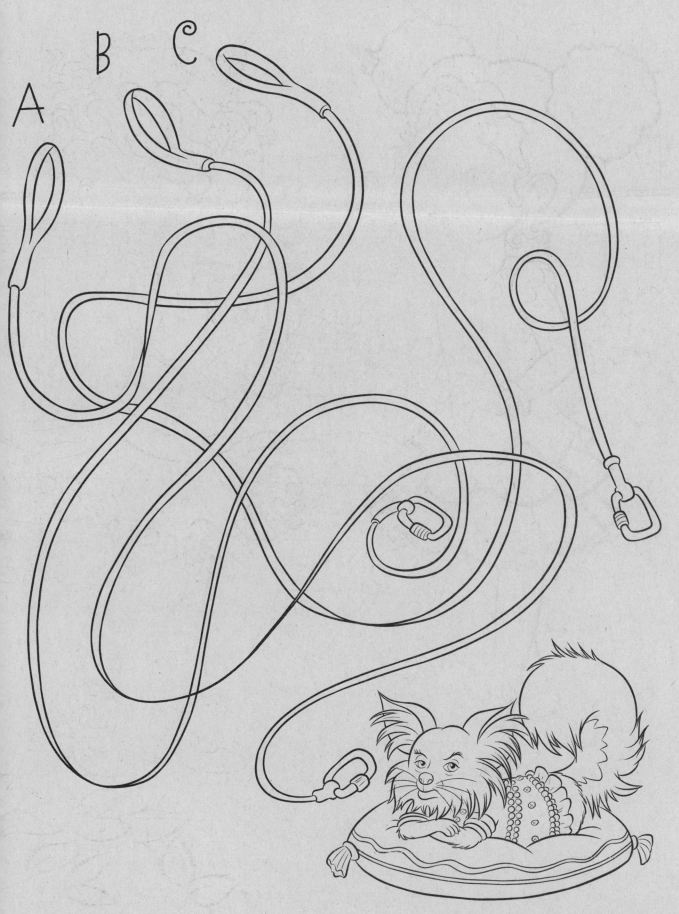

"I can picture the fanciest dog show . . ." I say.

What a dog!

Matching

Match the dogs to their shadows!

Answer:

Bree wants to enter Waffles in the dog show.

Bree gives Waffles some commands.

"Watch Frenchy follow my fancy commands," I say.

Rhyme Time

Circle the pictures of things that rhyme with pet.

"Frenchy, no!" I cry. "Sit. Stand. Stop!"

"Leap, Jewel!" says Mrs. Devine.

"Frenchy, if you want to win the show,
you have to be obedient," I say.

What's Different?

Find and circle seven things that are different in the second scene.

I try to get Frenchy to sit.
But he just wants to give kisses.

"Since you're a fancy dog, maybe we should start with a fancy trick," I say. "Frenchy, leap!"

"I'll show you how it's done," I say.
"I will *jeté*! That's fancy for leap!"

And, the Winner Is . . . .

Draw your own pet trophy!

My friends are ready for the dog show.

Wanda shows off the trophy!

Lionel and his dog, Flash, get in one last practice.

Unscramble the names!

FEWFLAS

_ _ _ _ _ _ _ _

CHRENFY

_ _ _ _ _ _ _

WEJLE

_ _ _ _ _

ASHLF

_ _ _ _ _

I think about Jewel. That's it!
I will borrow Jewel for the dog show!

I line up for the show with Jewel.
"Frenchy couldn't make it," I explain.

Jewel does everything perfectly!
"Ooh la la," I say. *"So fancy."*

Who Can It Be?

Connect the dots to see my favorite pet!

Jewel is about to do her fanciest trick yet
when I see Frenchy.

"I'm so sorry, Jewel," I say. "But my heart belongs to another… Frenchy, here, boy!"

"Oh, Frenchy," I say, laughing. "I missed you!"

Picture This . . . . .

Put the pictures in order by numbering them 1 to 4.

A____

B____

C____

D____

Answer: 1=B/ 2=C/ 3=D/ 4=A

Bree and Waffles win the show!

I don't care about winning as long as I have Frenchy.
"You're the best dog in the world!" I tell him.